David Bedford was born  southwest of England, in 196

David wasn't always a writ soccer player! He played for two teams: Appleton Football Club and Sankey Rangers. Although these weren't the worst teams in the league, they never won anything! David was also a scientist. His first job was in the United States, where he worked on discovering new antibiotics.

But, David always loved to read, and he decided to start writing stories himself. After a few years, he left his job as a scientist and began writing full-time. He now has over 15 books published, which have been translated into many languages around the world.

David lives with his wife and two children in Norfolk, England.

Keith Brumpton has written and illustrated over 35 humorous books for children. He also writes scripts and screenplays. Keith lives in Glasgow, Scotland.

For Ali and David, for all your
help and guidance.
DB

First American Edition 2006
by Kane/Miller Book Publishers, Inc.
La Jolla, California

First published in 2004 by Little Hare Books, Australia
Text copyright ©David Bedford 2004
Illustrations copyright ©Keith Brumpton 2004

Library of Congress Control Number: 2006920744
Printed and bound in China
1 2 3 4 5 6 7 8 9 10

ISBN-13: 978-1-933605-06-7
ISBN-10: 1-933605-06-5

DaVID BEDFORD

SUPERTEAM

Illustrated by KEith Brumpton

Kane/Miller
BOOK PUBLISHERS

Chapter 1

Harvey's fingers trembled as he handed over the money. He'd never seen so much in his life, and it was all his.

He tried to look relaxed while the shop assistant counted the handful of bills, but he began to sweat when she tipped out his piggy bank and started sorting his entire life savings into neat piles of coins. Was it enough? He'd checked it at least five times, but…

The shop assistant gave Harvey a small, grey padded case with a picture of an armadillo on the front.

He felt his face growing hot. It was Monday, the day before the new school year started, and the shop was packed with people who'd do anything to own what Harvey was holding. He was sure they were all staring at him greedily.

"Th-thanks!" Harvey stammered, tucking the case safely under his arm and walking quickly from the shop. As soon as he was outside, he put his head down and sprinted towards home. He'd done it! He, Harvey Boots, had just bought a pair of Armadillo Aces, the best football cleats anyone could buy.

Skidding into Baker Street, he saw his neighbor, Professor Gertie, leaning from the top window of her inventing tower.

"Bring them up right away!"she called.

Harvey pushed open the door to the tower and clambered up the twisting stairs to where Mark 1, the Soccer Machine, was waiting. He was Professor Gertie's greatest invention: a robot designed purely for playing soccer.

Mark 1 grabbed for the Armadillo box, but Harvey held it out of his reach.

"Awww," Mark 1 complained, in his strange, mechanical voice.

"Over here!" Professor Gertie was at her workbench. "I know how hard you saved for those cleats," she said.

"It would be a terrible shame to get them scuffed and muddy your first game. So, especially for you, I've invented PAP. It stands for Polish And Protect."

She held up a sprayer Harvey had seen her use to water plants. Now it had skull-and-crossbones danger signs on it.

Harvey's hands tightened on his Armadillos. Professor Gertie's inventions sometimes backfired. "Er, have you tested it?" he asked politely.

Professor Gertie tutted. "What do you think?" She raised a foot and showed him one of her ancient white sandals. They were usually grubby, but now they shone so brightly it hurt Harvey to look at them.

Harvey wanted to feel encouraged, but he had the urge to escape. How could he though? Professor Gertie did everything she could for The Team. She'd invented Mark 1 for them and, as their coach, he'd helped them win the league last season, and a trip to Soccer Camp.

"Don't worry," Professor Gertie said soothingly. "PAP is designed to help, not harm."

With a *whirr*, Mark 1 tugged the case away from Harvey, unzipped it, and tipped the jet black Armadillo Aces onto the table. Professor Gertie lined them up in a patch of sunlight.

"They're magnificent!" she declared. "Now stand back…"

Mark 1 made an urgent blaring noise like a warning siren and dove behind the sofa.

Harvey didn't move. He couldn't take his eyes off the small Armadillo badges on the side of each boot. They looked so perfect…

Professor Gertie sprayed twice.

Harvey saw a rainbow through the mist of oily droplets. As each drop landed on the Aces, it left a wet, glistening spot. Harvey bent closer. The spots began to pop, sizzle and crack.

He jerked backwards as puffs of smoke erupted like tiny mushroom clouds. There was a smell like cheese and toilet cleaner and rotten fish. Harvey held his nose and looked pleadingly at Professor Gertie. She goggled despairingly back at him.

"But you said you'd tested it!" shouted Harvey, coughing as the boots steamed, writhed and shriveled into two shapeless black blobs.

"I did!" cried Professor Gertie, "As soon as I made it! Yesterday!"

She unscrewed the top of the plant sprayer, sniffed, then slumped down onto her stool.

"What is it?" asked Harvey. "What happened?"

"It's gone bad," she said feebly. "Oh, Harvey, what have I done?"

Chapter 2

"Where are they?" asked Darren as Harvey joined him and Rita on the field that evening. "You said you were getting Armadillos."

"Really?" asked Rita, surprised. "But how can Harvey afford those?"

Harvey looked longingly at Darren's and Rita's cleats. They both had new Power Strikes – not too expensive, but good enough. Harvey wished he'd bought the same ones, and not let Professor Gertie anywhere near them.

He sighed, and told Darren and Rita what had happened. Rita gave a short, shocked gasp. Darren hid his face behind his goalkeeper's gloves.

"Wait," Rita said, frowning. "I still don't understand…"

"They're gone!" Darren wailed. "Professor Gertie blew up Harvey's Armadillos!"

"Not that bit," said Rita, putting her hands on her hips. "How did you get a pair of Armadillo Aces in the first place?" she asked Harvey sternly.

Darren lowered his gloves. "He didn't steal them, if that's what you mean," he said. "Harvey bought them."

"Armadillos cost a fortune!" said Rita.

"I used my savings," said Harvey quickly.

"But how did you save enough…?" Rita began.

"He got money for his birthday," interrupted Darren. "And he spent what his folks gave him to buy new school stuff."

"I'll just wear my old uniform again," Harvey explained. "I'm sure it will still fit."

"It better," said Rita doubtfully, "And what about your old cleats? Do they still fit?"

She pointed at the well-worn Power
Juniors Harvey had on.

"They're a bit tight," admitted Harvey,
crouching down to loosen the laces as the
rest of The Team arrived. It was their first
meeting to plan for the new season, and
Harvey saw that everyone on The Team had
new cleats. Most wore Power Strikes, but not
Steffi. Her cleats were glittery lilac, Harvey
noticed, and they had "Primadonna"
scrawled along the side. She had a second,
bright pink pair dangling from one shoulder.

"I prefer not to wear the same color every game," Harvey heard her explain to Matt.

Matt lifted a foot, and Harvey felt a shiver run through him when he saw the tiny Armadillo badge. "Aces are as good as three pairs in one," Matt announced. Then he looked down at Harvey's cleats. "You should get professional ones like these, Harv. You'd score more goals, easy. I don't know why you're still wearing Juniors."

"They're so yesterday," commented Steffi, wrinkling her nose as if Harvey's old cleats smelled bad.

"They look like something out of a museum," agreed Matt.

"Harvey feels comfortable in them, that's all," said Darren defensively. "They're your lucky cleats, aren't they, Harvey?"

Harvey didn't want to explain, so he nodded.

"Is this supposed to be our lucky uniform, too?" asked Steffi, pouting as she tried to smooth the creases from her shirt.

"We look like we've just crawled out of a washing machine, and I feel crumply."

The Team were wearing shirts, shorts and socks made from Professor Gertie's Supercloth, which was supposed to never need washing. The problem was, Professor Gertie hadn't tested it with water, and when their uniforms got wet for the first time at Soccer Camp, The Team had been lost under a mountain of soap bubbles.

"Everyone makes mistakes," Harvey said gloomily. "Anyway, she rinsed out the soap, so we should be okay."

"I suppose we're stuck with them then," sulked Steffi.

The Team passed a ball around to warm up. Every time Harvey kicked it though, his squashed-up toes felt like they were being hit with a hammer. He tried a gentle flick to Rita, and winced in pain.

Howls of laughter came from the side of the field where, Harvey saw with dismay, a crowd had gathered to watch. He recognized several players from other teams, including the captain of the Diamonds, Paul Pepper, who was in his class at school.

"Keep trying!" Paul Pepper jeered. "Practice makes perfect!"

"What are they doing here?" asked Harvey.

"Checking us out," said Rita. "We're the team to beat this year. After all, last season we came from the bottom to make it to the top of the league."

Aware that he was being watched, Harvey kicked the ball high towards Matt, and then crumpled to the ground, rolling in agony.

"I heard something snap!" Harvey yelped, gripping his left cleat as he heard the spectators cheering. Then, closer to him, he heard someone chuckling.

"It's not funny!" Harvey told Rita through clenched teeth.

"Sorry!" Rita spluttered. "It's just…" She pointed at Harvey's foot and began laughing so hard she couldn't speak.

Harvey sat up, and saw that his big toe was waving in the air. It had poked clean through his cleat and his sock. "So that's what made the snapping sound," he said, sighing.

Matt crouched beside him. "If you can wiggle it, it's not broken," he said knowledgeably.

Harvey wiggled his toe. "It's okay," he said.

"Phew!" said Rita. "The last thing we need at the start of the season is an injured captain."

"What we really need is a captain with a decent pair of cleats," said Steffi glumly.

Harvey glanced from his useless Juniors to The Team's worried faces.

Then he blushed as, led by Paul Pepper, the audience on the sidelines began singing, "Boot up, boot up, Har-vey Boots!"

Harvey stayed seated on the grass. He didn't feel like getting up; things could only get worse. Then he saw that one of the people from the sidelines was walking towards him.

"That's Jackie Spoyle," whispered Rita. "Her dad owns Spoyle's Sports Shop. She goes to your school, doesn't she?"

Harvey nodded. He'd bought his Armadillos from Spoyle's, and Jackie had been there, choosing what she was now wearing: a black warm-up suit with soccer balls all over it.

"She lives in that big house on my street," Rita told him, "and she gets everything she wants. Last year it was her own gym to work out in. The year before she got a horse and jumps. She always gets the best gear, too."

"Looks like she's decided to be a soccer ball now," said Darren.

Harvey began to laugh, and then stopped. He'd just seen Jackie Spoyle's silver cleats. They had armadillos on the side, but they weren't Aces.

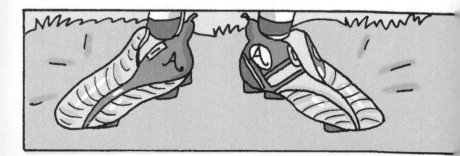

"These are Imps," Jackie told him. "They've only just come out and aren't even in the shops yet. But believe me, they're the best." She surveyed The Team, coughed lightly to clear her throat, and said, "I'm organizing a new squad of players. An elite squad."

It took Harvey a moment to realize what she meant, but before he could respond, Rita beat him to it. "You're not stealing anyone from The Team!" she said hotly.

"Get out of here!" snorted Matt, swatting the air as if he was shooing away a fly.

Jackie looked Matt up and down, making a face as if she'd tasted something nasty. "I will be hand-picking the most promising talent," she said. "Some of you will be hearing from me again. Others, alas, will not."

Matt cackled as she walked away, but Harvey noticed that Steffi was watching Jackie with interest. "It makes sense, when you think about it," Steffi muttered. "She's designing a team."

"Designer rubbish won't beat us," said Darren gruffly.

Harvey wasn't so sure. It all depended on who Jackie Spoyle could get to play for her – and what she had to attract them with.

Suddenly, Jackie spun around. "You do know you're all wrinkly, don't you?" she asked, smirking. "Anyone who joins me will have an all new uniform."

She unzipped her warm-up suit and Harvey heard his entire team gasp. Underneath, she was wearing a golden shirt, dazzling silver shorts and socks and, of course, the newest Armadillos.

Harvey couldn't take his eyes off them.

"Plus," Jackie continued, lifting one of her Imps to show off their gold-banded studs, "members of *my* team can choose anything else they need from my family's shop, for free."

Harvey heard a buzz of excitement, as if someone had stirred a beehive with a stick. Then someone called eagerly to Jackie, "What's your team called?"

"We're The Superteam," Jackie replied. "Didn't you know? You're playing us next Saturday…If The Team has any players left by then."

Chapter 3

"Look on the bright side," said Steffi. "Quality opposition means The Team will have to play better. It'll be good for us."

"But she wants to steal our players!" said Darren.

"And our name," said Harvey. "She's just putting 'super' in front of it, that's all."

"Jackie Spoyle might always get what she wants," said Rita, "but she's not getting The Team!" She snatched the ball from Matt and angrily kicked it into the air.

There was a silence, followed by a loud gong that sounded like someone had hit a trashcan with a baseball bat. Harvey turned and saw Mark 1 rubbing his head as he bounded over, his eyes flashing.

The robot put a powerful hand on Harvey's shoulder and began dragging him away. "Mine!" he bleated urgently. "MINE!"

Harvey jogged along beside Mark 1, trying not to catch his big toe in the grass, or stub it on the pavement. Darren and Rita followed behind.

"What's wrong?" Harvey kept asking, but Mark 1 didn't reply.

When they reached Baker Street, Harvey increased his pace. Something was going on at the inventing tower. As they drew closer, he saw a sign:

"For Sale! Amazing Inventions!"

Professor Gertie trudged from the tower door, her arms full of strange and wonderful-looking objects which she dropped with a crash onto her lawn.

Harvey heard Mark 1 start to tick rapidly, like a bomb about to go off.

"Have no fear!" Professor Gertie said when she spotted them. "By this time tomorrow, Harvey will be ankle-deep in Armadillos!"

Darren squatted down and grabbed an invention. It was the Shoosh! Gun that Harvey had seen Professor Gertie use to shoot nets over spiders. Rita poked delicately at some portable Lock Jaws, which were a new kind of safe.

"You won't have any problem selling these!" Darren said. "It's the first day of school tomorrow and nearly everyone walks past here."

"Do they really?" Professor Gertie asked, giving Harvey a knowing wink.

With a distressed *beep!*, Mark 1 let go of Harvey's arm, scooped up as many things as he could from the ground, and disappeared inside the tower with them. Harvey heard him clattering up the stairs at top speed.

Professor Gertie sighed loudly. "For some reason, that robot thinks all my useless gadgets belong to him. His bedroom is packed full of them!"

"You mean these are all Mark 1's?" asked Rita.

"Don't worry," said Professor Gertie. "There's nothing here of any real value."

Harvey couldn't believe what he was hearing. "I'm not having any cleats bought with Mark 1's stuff!" he said, looking to Rita and Darren for support.

"It's totally unfair," agreed Rita. "But then again…" she bit her lip. "We won't beat The Superteam if you have to play in your socks, will we?"

"You're our captain," said Darren firmly. "If you can't play your best, The Team won't hold together. You need cleats, Harvey."

"And I ruined your Armadillos," said Professor Gertie. "So you have to let me buy you another pair."

Harvey shook his head, but didn't say anything.

"To tell you the truth," Professor Gertie said brightly, "I'm quite enjoying myself. It's about time my inventions started earning me some cash!"

She skipped merrily back inside the tower.

"Mark 1 shouldn't have to suffer," Harvey told Darren and Rita. "If there were any other way of getting new cleats, I'd take it."

"Well, there is one possibility," said Rita. "You could borrow Steffi's spare pair."

Darren was aghast. "But they're pink!"

Rita retreated down Baker Street, pulling Darren along with her.

"Pink cleats are better than no cleats," Rita insisted.

"Don't do it, Harvey!" Darren cried.

Darren was right, Harvey thought. There was no way his reputation would survive if he was seen wearing pink cleats.

That night, Harvey stayed up late, watching through his bedroom window as Professor Gertie carried inventions from her tower, and Mark 1 bundled them straight back inside again. The robot was now making furious popping noises and giving off steam.

Then, around ten o'clock, Harvey heard a high-pitched *BEEEEeeeeeeeeep!* followed by silence. Mark 1 didn't emerge from the tower again.

Harvey felt uneasy as he crawled into bed and began rubbing his sore toes. He didn't know what he was going to do. The Team needed him, but so did Mark 1.

As he drifted off to sleep, he was only sure of one thing – he would stand and face The Superteam on Saturday, even if he had to play barefoot. Nobody was going to take over The Team.

Chapter 4

A girl was shrieking, "I'm having it, and there's nothing you can do about it!"

Harvey's eyes snapped open. Darting to his window, he saw that it was morning, and Professor Gertie's Amazing Inventions Sale was in full swing.

Harvey hurriedly searched for the pants and sweater he'd worn to school last year, and tugged them on. Everything felt tight and short, and he couldn't even get his shoes on his feet until he had loosened the laces as far as they would go.

"One at a time!" he heard Professor Gertie holler. "If you fight over them, you'll break them!"

Harvey left his house at full speed and jumped over the fence into Professor Gertie's garden. He dodged a group of small boys who were stuck together with Velcro Balls, and spotted Professor Gertie sitting at a table facing a long line of shoppers.

Harvey groaned. He was too late. Nearly all her inventions had sold already. He looked around for Mark 1, but couldn't see him.

A girl next to him held up a pile of paper. "What's this?" she asked.

"Aha," said Professor Gertie. "That's my Rub-a-Dub paper!"

Harvey watched her press a piece of the plain paper onto her open notebook. When she peeled it off, she'd made an exact copy.

"It's for homework!" the girl squealed. Professor Gertie began to sell the Rub-a-Dub paper one sheet at a time.

Darren arrived, looking pleased. "At this rate she'll have the money to buy your cleats in no time," said Darren. "Come on, we're late."

As they walked down the hill, Harvey felt cool air around his wrists and ankles. He tried pulling his sleeves down, but they sprang back up again. Then, as they turned into the school grounds, he was met by a chorus of giggling girls. Jackie Spoyle was standing with her friends, blocking the path.

"Look everyone," said Jackie. "This year Harvey Boots is setting the style!"

Harvey blushed as Jackie's gang shrieked with laughter.

Darren barged through them, making a gap so that Harvey could follow.

"Steffi says Harvey *likes* old things," Jackie went on. "He doesn't look very comfortable in them though!"

Darren turned on her. "What have you been talking to Steffi for?"

"I've been chatting to all the league's stars," Jackie said primly. "I do wish Steffi went to our school. She's got the right kind of attitude, doesn't she? And Rita, too, she's *very* keen."

Darren's face turned fiery red, but before he could say anything else, Harvey hustled him into their classroom. "Forget about it," Harvey said. "Rita would never play for her."

Darren collapsed onto a chair at the back of the class. "Maybe not," he said. "But some of the others might. Steffi's always complaining that we don't have a cool uniform. She'll be the first to go."

Throughout the morning, Harvey and Darren tried to work out who would be tempted to join The Superteam. They had plenty of time to talk. Their teacher, Mr. Spottiwoode, was trying to keep the class from rioting.

"I hope Professor Gertie doesn't get into trouble for this," Harvey said as a boy near them used the Shoosh! Gun to fire nets over himself until his hair looked like it was covered in thick, stringy cobwebs.

Darren was batting away bubbles. "Where are these coming from?" he asked. One burst over him. "Hey! They stink!"

"It must be Professor Gertie's Blow Off," Harvey explained. "It captures smells inside bubbles. Rekha's using it."

By the end of the day, Mr. Spottiwoode's desk was piled high with confiscated inventions, and Darren was busy scribbling a list of all the players The Team were likely to lose.

He showed it to Harvey on their way home.

"You've written down everyone but me and you!" said Harvey.

"We're the only ones I can be absolutely sure of," said Darren.

"What about Rita?"

Darren grimaced. "We can't be certain…"

"Yes, we can," said Harvey, and he scratched off Rita's name. Then he noticed a large crowd gathered around Professor Gertie's tower.

"What's going on?" he asked, breaking into a run. "I thought she sold everything this morning."

Darren jumped up to see over people's heads. "Looks like she's found a few tons more. Mark 1's bedroom must have been jam-packed!"

They pushed their way through, and found Professor Gertie weighing an ancient handbag in her hands. It made a dull rattle just like the sound Harvey's piggy bank had made when it was full.

Professor Gertie waved when she saw Harvey. "If I keep my sale going all week, we should have enough money for your cleats by Friday."

"All week?" asked Harvey dismally. "How many more inventions do you have left to sell?"

"Thousands," purred Professor Gertie, rubbing her hands together.

"How's Mark 1?" Harvey asked hopefully. "Is he feeling better?"

"He won't get out of bed," said Professor Gertie. "He normally only does that when he's thinking very hard, but this time he seems to have turned himself off!"

Harvey felt terrible. Mark 1 had never turned himself off before! Harvey had to tell Professor Gertie to stop the sale. There was no way he could accept cleats bought in this way.

"I'm not…" he started to say, and then he was knocked off his feet as a crush of shoppers suddenly surged forward.

He just had time to see someone holding up what looked like a hard hat with helicopter blades before he crawled away on his hands and knees.

"I've got an idea," Darren said excitedly as Harvey stood up. "The Team's practice sessions are always on Thursday nights, right?"

"Yeah," Harvey sighed, "so what?"

"So, the people who turn up on Thursday will see that The Team's captain still doesn't have cleats, and they might decide to join Spoyle's team after all."

"There's nothing we can do about it,"
said Harvey.

"There is," said Darren. "I'll call everyone
and change the practice session to Friday."
He grinned. "When they see your Armadillos,
there's no way they'll give up on The Team!"

As he watched Darren jog home, Harvey
felt his own energy drain away. He slouched
into his house and up to his room.

"I'm not going to wear Professor Gertie's
Armadillos," he decided finally.

There had to be some other way of
keeping The Team together. Harvey curled up
in bed and began to think very hard.

He was soon snoring noisily.

Chapter 5

The rest of the week seemed to Harvey like a game everyone else was playing while he sat on the sidelines and watched.

On Wednesday, Professor Gertie's sale was busier than the day before, Jackie and her friends welcomed him to school with a well-practiced cheer, Darren talked constantly about the new Armadillos Harvey would be getting, and Mr. Spottiwoode spent the whole day pouncing on Professor Gertie's inventions.

On Thursday morning, the sale was still busy; Jackie and her friends applauded Harvey when he arrived at school, and Mr. Spottiwoode lost part of his moustache when a hungry Frizz Bee landed on his nose.

"They're for trimming knotted bits of hair, actually," Harvey heard Rekha explain to her friend, "definitely not for moustaches."

Harvey's spirits rose briefly on Thursday afternoon.

He scored with one of his best-ever swerving free kicks on the playground, and Jackie Spoyle was watching.

"That will give her something to think about!" Darren shouted, adding to Harvey, "You'll be unstoppable once you've got your Armadillos."

At last, on Friday morning, Harvey began to feel some relief. Professor Gertie, who looked exhausted, was no longer bringing out more inventions from her tower. And when Harvey got to school, Jackie and her friends were nowhere in sight.

"When Spoyle saw you score yesterday, she got worried," Darren reported later that afternoon. "She's now promising The Superteam free tickets to professional games, a real soccer coach, and an all-expenses-paid international summer tournament!"

Harvey felt like he'd been kicked in the stomach. "How can we compete with that?" he asked despairingly.

"Easy," said Darren. "First, you get your Armadillos. That will help most of The Team decide to stay with us. Then we hammer The Superteam into the ground."

Harvey saw a triumphant glint in Darren's eyes, and knew he was going to let his friend down badly. He wouldn't be wearing Armadillos, and it was about time he told Darren.

Suddenly, Harvey heard a long, agonized scream, and saw Paul Pepper waving his hand violently in the air, trying to dislodge a pair of Lock Jaws.

"What on earth is that?" demanded Mr. Spottiwoode.

"I keep my pencils in it," said the shy boy who sat next to Paul Pepper. He keyed a code into the base of the Lock Jaw, and Paul Pepper's hand was released. "I bought it from the professor who lives next door to Harvey Boots," the boy said. "That's where *all* these weird things come from."

The bell began to ring for the end of the day, and Harvey and Darren ducked their heads and bolted from the room. "Let's get the money, then go to Spoyle's to buy your Armadillos," urged Darren.

They ran through the school gates and onto Baker Street where Harvey tugged on Darren's arm to make him stop. "I can't do it," he said. "That money belongs to Mark 1, and he should have it."

Harvey looked into his friend's face, expecting Darren to be devastated, or at least upset. But to his surprise, Darren smiled with satisfaction.

"Brilliant idea!" he said, blinking rapidly as he worked it out. "Mark 1 gets the cash, and then we ask him to do what he was invented for: saving The Team."

Harvey was confused. Had Darren forgotten? "The referees won't let robots play," Harvey reminded him.

Darren shook his head. "I didn't mean that. All Mark 1 has to do is buy you some Armadillos!"

Harvey thought about it and began to feel excited. Of course Mark 1 would want to help them! "Let Mark 1 choose what to do," Harvey decided.

"If he wants to get me some cleats, I'll wear them. But I'll pay him back. I don't care how long it takes. I could even buy back some of Professor Gertie's inventions for him..."

Darren sneezed. "What's that smell?"

Harvey sniffed, and the memory of melting Armadillos came back to him like a nightmare he couldn't forget. He glanced up and saw a wisp of smoke rising from beside the inventing tower.

They found Professor Gertie standing in her garden, as still as a statue, holding the plant sprayer with the skull-and-crossbones stickers. On the path next to her, a pair of Armadillo Aces were on fire.

"I made it fresh," she said weakly, giving the sprayer a tiny shake. "I decided to buy your cleats for you as a surprise, and I was rushing to have them ready and…Oh, Harvey, I must have made a mistake when I mixed the formula!"

"Not again!" said Darren. "Wait a minute, how much of the money did you spend?"

"*All* of it!" whimpered Professor Gertie.

"There's nothing else we can do then," said Darren, holding his head in his hands. "I give up!"

Chapter 6

Harvey and Darren met Rita on the field that night. While they waited for the others to arrive, Darren told her about the new Armadillos.

"I know that Professor Gertie means well," Rita said, speaking very, very quietly. "But sometimes," she said, her voice rising, "I wish she would stop trying to MAKE THINGS BETTER!"

"Me too," said Harvey.

"Me three," said Darren grumpily.

"And where is everyone?" Rita snapped, when it was clear that nobody else was going to turn up. "I thought Matt would stay with us, at least."

"You did tell everyone that the practice session had changed to tonight, didn't you?" Harvey checked with Darren.

Darren slapped his forehead with his gloved hand.

"You mean you didn't?!" cried Rita. "But hang on, you told *me*!"

"I was too busy persuading the others not to join The Superteam!" said Darren. "I just forgot!"

"But that means that anyone else who wanted to stay on The Team would have shown up *yesterday*!" cried Rita.

"And because we weren't there," said Harvey, "they'll think we've joined Jackie's team. So they'll probably join too!"

Friday night practice was over.

It was dark when Harvey arrived home.
Someone was waiting outside his house.

"Here's what you need," said Jackie
Spoyle.

Harvey could barely see what she was
giving him, but he knew the feel of
Armadillos as he held them in his hands.
And these weren't Aces. They were lighter,
and more supple, and...

"They're your size," said Jackie. "I'm
captain of The Superteam – but tomorrow,
you can be our striker."

Harvey didn't hear her leave. He was busy
getting used to his Imps.

Chapter 7

Harvey left his house on a cloudy Saturday morning carrying a shopping bag.

"You were right, and I was wrong," said Professor Gertie, who was trying to fix her trampled flowerbeds. "I should never have taken away Mark 1's things. He won't come out of his room, or let me in, and I know he's up to something in there."

"You did what you thought was best," said Harvey.

Professor Gertie wasn't listening to him. "I wish I could give his things back. There *is* one thing I didn't sell." She pointed to a shadow behind the tower door.

Harvey took a step closer to see what it was, then cringed. Icy shivers ran up and down his spine.

It was Masher, the monstrous waste disposal machine that Professor Gertie had made to eat inventions that didn't work.

Harvey once had a nightmare where Masher was trying to catch him. Now, looking into the killer machine's beady eyes, he wondered if he really had been dreaming. Its rows of jagged teeth were gnawing on the chain that secured it to a metal ring on the wall, and its crab-like claw was nipping chunks out of a sign that said:

"*Weird Pet For Sale! (Pat him, he's friendly!)*"

"Y-you've got to be joking!" spluttered Harvey.

"People are always on the look-out for something different," said Professor Gertie. "And Masher would make an ideal family companion. He likes children; he only needs oiling once a week, and he eats any old junk."

Harvey eyed Masher warily, as he would a dog that was known to bite. A noise like stones being crushed came from deep inside the creature's mechanical jaws.

"His growl is worse than his bite," said Professor Gertie. "His teeth are worn down, and his claw is blunt, the poor dear."

Harvey was about to tell Professor Gertie that she couldn't let Masher loose on innocent people, when he realized he had nothing to worry about. There was no way anybody would want Masher.

"I have to go," said Harvey. "And don't worry about my cleats anymore; it's taken care of."

When he reached the field, Harvey saw The Team mingling with about twenty other players. He recognized most of them; they were nearly all the league's best goal scorers.

Jackie hadn't picked a single defender, and Harvey guessed that The Superteam defense was going to be useless.

He spotted Jackie modeling The Superteam's gold and silver uniform. Behind her there was a neat pile of Armadillo boxes. The Superteam players were going to be equipped with the finest of everything, just as Jackie had promised.

Harvey strolled up to her.

"Hi, Striker," said Jackie. "I'm glad you're with us." She unfolded a golden shirt and draped it over his shoulders. "This is for you," she said, beaming.

Harvey lifted the Imps from his bag. He saw Darren and Rita standing side by side, with their mouths open in disbelief.

"No thanks," Harvey said to Jackie. "I have a team already. These are for you."

Jackie's smile vanished as he gave her back the Imps. She snatched back the shirt. "You *lose*, Harvey Boots," she spat after him as he turned his back on her. "You've already *lost*."

Harvey, Darren and Rita headed arm in arm towards the field. Harvey's heart was thumping. This was it. If the rest of The Team didn't follow, they really would have lost before the game even started.

Steffi strode past them. "Come on," she said angrily, "let's show Superbrat what a *real* team can do!"

Matt trotted closely behind her. "Poor Steffi!" he said quietly. "She wasn't part of Spoiled's designs; she was only asked to be their *substitute*!"

Harvey watched with pride as The Team took their positions on the field.

"I don't get it," said Darren. "Everyone is here!"

"Of course they are," said Rita. "We're The Team, remember? Teams are teams because they stick together, no matter what."

Harvey, though, noticed that some of his teammates were frowning at his well-worn school shoes.

"These are fine," he told everyone. "I play in them every day."

"On grass?" asked Steffi.

"No," said Harvey, "but…"

"In the rain?" asked Steffi as a dark cloud bathed them in shadow.

Harvey didn't answer her. "If it rains," he muttered to Rita, "my shoes are going to slide all over the place."

"It won't rain," Rita said confidently.

The teams faced each other. The Superteam team members who weren't playing this time stood on the sidelines wearing golden baseball caps and chanting their support.

The referee blew her whistle, and Harvey kicked off, just as a cold drop of rain landed on his nose.

"That cloud doesn't have more than an eggcup of rain in it," said Rita carelessly as she returned the ball to him.

Heavy drops began falling on Harvey's head. He back-heeled the ball to Steffi, then ran into the empty space to receive it.

But as he reached out his left leg, his right foot slipped, tumbling him to the grass. Rita gathered the ball and headed for The Superteam's goal. Harvey could hardly see her through the downpour, and the next thing he knew, a Superteam player was trying to set up an attack.

Harvey closed in on her fast, stuck out his foot to intercept the ball, then skidded, tripped and dove headfirst into her stomach, knocking her flat on her back.

The ref stood over Harvey, showing him a yellow card. "Outrageous foul!" she said furiously. "One more like that and I'm sending you off!"

Harvey slipped twice more as he limped to the side of the field. The rain was stopping, but the grass was already soaked and muddy.

"Keep out of the action until it dries," Rita advised him.

Harvey watched helplessly as the game went on in front of him. His absence was putting The Team under pressure, but Harvey was encouraged by how they responded.

Rita dropped back into defense, and they built their forward moves slowly so that The Superteam couldn't break through them on the counterattack. The problem was, The Team were unable to finish their attacks; without Harvey, they didn't have a natural goal-scorer, but The Superteam had plenty.

Harvey watched Paul Pepper gather the ball and set a straight course for Darren's goal, skipping past one Team player after another.

"Tackle him!" Harvey bellowed. Matt, Steffi and Rita lunged for the ball, but Paul Pepper still managed to shoot.

Darren dove at full stretch, pushed the ball onto the post with his fingertips, and slid along the grass, leaving the goal undefended. Harvey put up his arms to celebrate the save, and then saw Jackie trot up to the ball. All she had to do was walk it into the net, and with a grin of triumph, she did.

Harvey watched in frustration as Jackie
Spoyle did a victory dance in front of him.
He felt desperate. He had to play somehow.

Then he saw Mark 1 racing across the
field, balancing a tattered picnic basket on
his head and calling urgently, "Cleeeeets!"

Chapter 8

Mark 1 set the picnic basket on the ground, and Harvey rummaged through a jumbled mass of string, a sink plunger, yogurt cups with smiley faces painted on the sides, old corks, a tea strainer, and two egg cartons packed with grey powder.

"Is there something here for me?" Harvey asked.

"Cleeeeets!!" said the robot, nodding happily.

Harvey searched again. He heard The Superteam cheer as they scored a second goal, and he began to panic. "Where are they?" he asked anxiously. "Which cleats?"

Mark 1 bent down and unraveled the strung-together objects. Then he wrapped them around Harvey's shoes. He pulled the strings tight, tied a complicated knot, and held Harvey's hand as he tried to balance on the wobbly egg cartons.

Harvey didn't know what to say. The Superteam were celebrating their third goal, and he was standing on trash.

He took a step. After all, he told himself, Mark 1 had made them for him. The least he could do was try them.

Mark 1 shoved him onto the field just as the ball came bouncing their way.

Harvey took huge strides towards it. Concentrating on not falling over, he didn't hear the whistle for halftime. Instead, he lined himself up to kick the ball, drew back his left foot, and…the egg cartons exploded.

"Aaargh!" cried Harvey as he flew into the air, flapped his arms wildly, and crashed to the ground.

The Team wandered over as Harvey kicked off his burning shoes. Mark 1 snatched them up, tutting as he examined them.

"Looks like I'm playing in my bare feet," said Harvey as he quickly rolled off his smoldering socks.

A pair of pink Primadonnas fell into his lap. He looked up to see Steffi's embarrassed but determined face. "It's our only chance," she said.

Harvey heard The Superteam and their supporters start chanting, "Boot up, boot up, Har-vey Boots!" Jackie was laughing so hard her teeth reminded him of Professor Gertie's Lock Jaws.

"Don't even think about it," Darren warned, shaking his finger at Steffi's cleats as if he were scolding them. "Just…don't."

But Harvey knew it was their only hope. He put them on, stood up, and saw Professor Gertie marching towards him, holding a Spoyle Sports shoe box.

"No!" Harvey exclaimed, feeling like everything around him was going wrong, wrong, wrong. "You can't have sold Masher!"

"Even better than that," said Professor Gertie.

"But he's *dangerous!*" Harvey roared.

"Mr. Spotty? Oh, I wouldn't say he was *that* bad," said Professor Gertie in surprise.

"Mr. Spotty?" Harvey asked, bewildered.

"Your *teacher*," explained Professor Gertie.

"Mr. Spottiwoode bought Masher?" asked Darren.

"Of course he didn't," said Professor Gertie. "He came to ask about my inventions."

"Are you in trouble?" Harvey asked seriously.

"Quite the opposite," said Professor Gertie. "Your wonderful Mr. Spotty wants to buy thirty Lock Jaws!"

"What does he want those for?" asked Darren.

"He wants everyone in his class to have a secure pencil case," said the Professor. "Mr. Spotty said he'll be able to start his lessons on time if he doesn't have to find all the lost pencils and pens first."

"And he *paid* you for them?" asked Darren in astonishment.

"Yes!" cried Professor Gertie delightedly. "Although," she continued, "he only gave me a little bit to start with, and it wasn't enough to buy the cleats you wanted, Harvey. I could only afford the cheapest pair."

"*Any* will do," said Harvey with relief as Professor Gertie handed him a pair of ordinary black cleats.

"Don't worry," the professor said, leaning close so that only Harvey could hear.

"I stopped by the tower on the way here and fixed them up a bit."

Harvey groaned and hung his head, wishing that, just for once, Professor Gertie wouldn't interfere. Everything she'd invented for him lately had been a disaster.

"Aren't you going to try them?" she asked.

Harvey shrugged. He put on the new cleats carefully, handed Steffi back her Primadonnas, and walked to the edge of the center circle, taking small, delicate steps.

His feet felt cool and airy. Without thinking, he bounced up and down to get ready, then stopped. His toes had begun to tingle.

"Are you all right?" asked Rita. "You look scared!"

Harvey didn't reply. He heard the ref blow her whistle to start the second half, and felt his body tense up expectantly. He had no idea what would happen next.

Chapter 9

The Superteam kicked off and Rita chased for the ball. Harvey didn't move. His feet had suddenly become warm.

"Move it, Harvey!" called Matt, threading the ball to him. Harvey automatically took a step forward and intercepted it, feeling his cleats respond just like ordinary cleats should. The only difference was that these were so snug they felt like his feet's second skin.

Harvey was too nervous to kick the ball, so he used the side of his foot to roll it back to Steffi, and was surprised to see that it arrived exactly where he'd intended. Seeing a gap, he burst through, collected the ball on the run and stroked it gently ahead of him. Now he had a chance for a long shot.

"Shoot!" yelled Professor Gertie.

Harvey slowed down, waiting for his cleats to do something they shouldn't. What *had* Professor Gertie done to them?

He nudged the ball again. Nothing happened. The Superteam defenders were closing in, but he still had time to shoot. If only Professor Gertie's inventions didn't *always* catch fire, or blow up, or melt or just not work.

Well, some of the time her ideas *almost* worked...

"SHOOOOT!" insisted Mark 1.

With a mighty yell, Harvey put his trust in Professor Gertie.

He blasted the ball towards The Superteam's goal, watching it take off like a missile, skimming the grass, and spinning to the left. The goalkeeper dove low and got both hands to it, but he couldn't stop it.

"Goal!"

As the rest of The Team and their two supporters celebrated, Harvey took a close look at his left cleat. It still looked normal. "I don't believe it," he said, confused.

"Neither do I," said the ref suspiciously, pressing Harvey's cleat with her thumbs. "You haven't got a lump of steel in here, have you?"

"I dunno," said Harvey. "I mean, no, they're not heavy."

The ref examined his other cleat before restarting the game.

They felt alive, a part of him that did whatever he wanted them to do. He couldn't imagine what Professor Gertie had done to them, but he was sure of one thing; this time, her invention was a spectacular success.

Harvey sailed in a cross, and Rita thundered the ball into the net with her head. "Goal!"

Harvey did a back flip that fooled The Superteam defense, leaving the way open for Matt to trickle the ball home. "Goal!"

Harvey sent the ball curling from a free kick for his second goal, and soon after made his hat trick directly from a corner kick. "Goal! Goal!"

"Am I dreaming?" asked Darren, snatching off a glove so he could pinch himself.

"This is pathetic!" Harvey heard Paul Pepper whine as Steffi headed the ball through the goalie's legs. "You call this a super team? We might as well give up."

Other players from Jackie's team nodded their heads in agreement.

"Play on!" Jackie ordered. "I say when we give up!"

Harvey put his foot on the ball and watched as Paul Pepper wrenched off his top and threw it at her. "I don't like your style!" he hollered. "This isn't a team at all!"

"I know it's a bit early," said the ref hurriedly, "but we might as well call it a day." She blew the final whistle and said, "The Team wins six to three!"

Harvey tore down the field with his arms in the air and saw Darren staring at him with a look of terror on his face.

"What's wro-" Harvey began. Then, he heard the sound of grinding metal behind him. He spun around.

Masher's feet were pounding deep holes in the grass as he came at Harvey, teeth whizzing like chainsaws, claw snapping, and bitten-through chain whipping the air.

Harvey dove out of the way, rolled onto his knees, and looked around. Masher continued past him across the field, with Professor Gertie trailing behind.

"Mashy!" she cooed gently, "Here, Mashy!"

Masher reached The Superteam, his eyes rocking back and forth as if looking for someone. Harvey heard Paul Pepper bellow, "Your Superteam are JUNK!"

Suddenly, Masher darted forward. Jackie screamed as the metal monster pinched off one of her Armadillo Imps with his claw. Still screaming, she sprinted across the field.

Rita giggled. "Looks like Mashy's got the munchies!"

"But why did he pick on Spoyle?" asked Darren.

"Because," laughed Harvey, "he eats any old junk!"

Professor Gertie dashed after Masher and pulled him back by his chain. Then she gave Mark 1 a one-armed hug.

"That means sorry," she said. "From now on, anything I make that doesn't work is yours forever."

"He'll need an aircraft hanger to store it all," said Darren under his breath.

Professor Gertie put Masher's chain into Mark 1's hand and asked, "How would you like a weird pet?"

The robot's eyes flickered as he bent down to stroke the wire bristles on Masher's back. Masher made a purring noise, and Harvey covered his ears. The sound was horrible.

"Professor Gertie, what did you do to Harvey's cleats?" Rita wanted to know. "I mean, they were fantastic!"

"*Harvey* was fantastic," said Professor Gertie, prying off Harvey's left cleat. "All I did was...this!"

She pulled out a big wad of cotton balls. "They didn't have these cleats in Harvey's size," she explained, "so I had to stuff the toes to make them fit."

Harvey gasped. "Is that *all*? I thought…"

Professor Gertie smiled. "You didn't think I was going to let you down, did you?" she asked innocently.

Harvey looked around. Darren and Rita were always with him, of course. But so were the rest of The Team, and that included Mark 1 and Professor Gertie. They stuck together, no matter what.

Harvey grinned at Professor Gertie. "You? Let me down?" He started to laugh. "Never!"

Professor
Gertie

Darren

Harvey

Rita

Matt

Steffi

Mark 1